QUEEN OF THE CROSSROADS

A WORLDSBRIDGE ROAD'S BELOVED STORY

ERICA ANOE

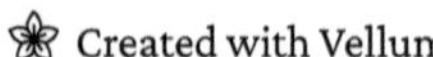
Created with Vellum

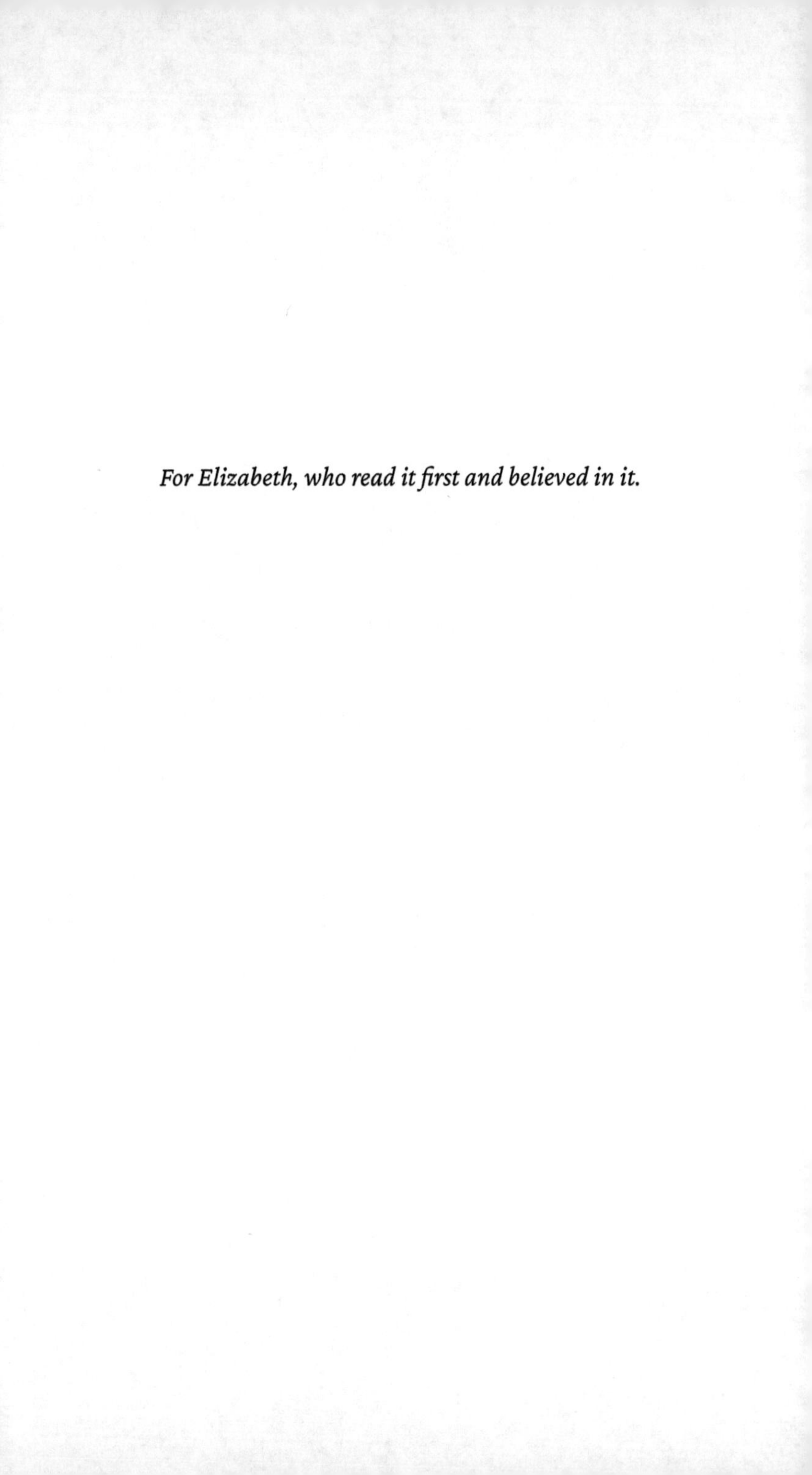

For Elizabeth, who read it first and believed in it.

I learn by going where I have to go.

— THEODORE ROETHKE

1

Entering a city resembled emerging from underwater. Passing through a city gate into streets that local residents saw as teeming with life was to set foot in an emptier, lonelier place. Sometimes Piper found it a relief – the thick and constant contact of magic along the Road took its toll – but it amused her that these cosmopolitans knew so little of what a full world really looked and felt like.

She unwound protective layers of cloth, slowly revealing her face, throat and arms. She watched the city guards around her react to the tangle of birthmarks on her uncovered skin, a personal map that recorded the gifts of every Road she'd ever walked and would ever walk. "You act like you've never seen a Road's Beloved." She laughed. "Surely, the city of Worldsbridge has sent and received messengers on more than one occasion."

Still, they shrank away, until one woman braved a reply. "We've never seen one so... covered."

"Ah, well if you saw me uncovered, you'd know exactly

how covered I am." She winked, enjoyed the answering blush.

A male guard, whose spear had dipped momentarily in the general consternation at Piper's appearance, cleared his throat and restored the rectitude of his posture. "You have a message?"

"No, I'm here to collect one."

It was a bit unusual for those of her kind to arrive in a city empty handed – the Road's magic normally displayed a love of efficiency. Piper, however, possessed knowledge of a hundred times the roads of the average Road's Beloved on a conservative estimate. The Road seemed to enjoy sending her on long, strange trips to places almost no one else knew how to reach, and that fundamentally whimsical quality manifested also in the message-carrying that most people associated with a Road's Beloved.

She removed her shoes and hung them carefully on the city gate. The dust of Road and dust of City could never mix except on the surface of her skin. Her kind had been coming here for years – other sets of shoes swung beside hers, some so ancient that it seemed they would fall to dust if she brushed them with a fingertip.

She offered a pleasant smile. "Where will I bathe? I'll need an attendant and clothing appropriate for court that I can put on afterward. I'll also need fresh shoes. The ruler of this place has a message for me."

"The King?" The city guards all glanced at each other nervously.

"He may not know it yet. That happens sometimes."

"The King hasn't spoken to anyone in years."

Piper widened her smile. "Well, he'll be speaking to me shortly. Let's prepare for it properly, shall we?" She pointed to the city guard with the cute blush. “You’ll do for an attendant unless someone objects. No? Let’s go.”

2

The best part of a city was the satiation it could provide. A chance to truly rest with no feeling of danger, to eat a meal in peace, to become entirely clean, to dirty oneself joyfully by making love to an attractive stranger, and then to bathe again. Piper took her time preparing for this visit to the apparently reclusive King, but at a certain point the lovely city guard was more than spent, and Piper's particular genius lay in never having overstayed her welcome, not even once in her life.

She stood and stretched luxuriously, accepting the guard's help winding her into corsetry and other silly city clothes, smiling indulgently at the way the guard's hands still trembled. When Piper was dressed, she pulled the guard into one last passionate kiss. "Darling–"

"Etta."

"I won't remember that, but it's nothing personal. You are beautiful, and you've given me a heavenly welcome to Worldsbridge, and that I will remember. You'll remember it, too. We won't see each other again."

"Not even..." A shy hand traced Piper's upper arm. "Not even on your way out?"

She shook her head. "You've seen another Road's Beloved, I assume?"

Etta nodded.

"Then you know that for most of them, their Road is contained, usually a polygonal design – a route, if you will."

"There are some who go back and forth between here and Sharksbay."

"Yes, exactly." Piper held out her hand, traced the complex, tangled line that meandered between her fingers and onto her palm. "I, on the other hand, have never found a spot where my road crossed over itself or doubled back. Every patch of ground I set foot on is new to me."

Etta's face fell, but Piper shook her head.

"It's better that way, I promise. I'm very grouchy in the mornings." She took Etta by the shoulders and turned her toward the way they'd come. "I do have one last gift for you, my lovely. For a little while after I've touched you, you become like me. If you find a mark on yourself afterward, it may even be for longer. This means that, if you like, you can go outside the city. For a little while. See what's out there."

"You mean that?" Etta breathed.

Piper smiled to herself. She always chose well. "Yes, but go quickly. You'll feel it when you need to return, and you must obey the feeling or it won't go well for you."

"Thank you," Etta said, "for everything." But Piper made sure to slip out of the room in the moments between the words so no further embrace was possible.

3

The area around the palace had fallen too quiet. Piper's new sandals smacked like hungry lips against the sandstone approach. She noted the arrows nocked in windows above, their deadly tips all trained on her.

She paid them no mind, for her Road unmistakably drew her to the ornately carved and intricately locked palace door. Piper knocked boldly.

"You were not summoned, Road's Beloved," a forbidding voice hissed through a slit in the door.

Piper laughed. "My kind is neither summoned nor sent away. My Road has carried me here, where there is a message for me. You will not like what happens should you become an obstacle in my path."

The door remained unmoved, so she put a hand on it. It recoiled from her, as if the very wood knew it had offended. Piper permitted herself a smile at the grunt of pain from the guard who had tried to refuse her entry. "You'll want to cool that before it bruises – and take a lesson from it."

She stepped into the palace. The hallways dripped with chilly silence and seemed to shudder at her every footstep. Dust motes were so thick in the air that she sneezed three times in quick succession. Lazy ceiling fans covered in layers of dust swirled so slowly that they disturbed nothing.

Piper walked past row upon row of portraits, noting the descent of their subjects from the conquering poses of warriors to the complacent smiles of those who fed on the labor of others. She saw barely a soul – the occasional whisper of a servant, more a retreating garment than an actual person, or the clank of a guard shifting position.

She came at last to a throne room, pushed the great doors open with a shoulder. Because of who she was, the hinges didn't protest when she forced them to move.

The room she revealed would have been grander were it not so gray and faded. The carpet there may once have been red. Suits of armor stood in oddly relaxed attitudes, their previously martial positions eased by time like guards grown lax from lack of supervision.

A man sat on the throne, so enveloped in pillows that his form was hard to make out in the dim light. Blankets and clothing covered all but the backs of his hands and his face, and what skin did show was ashy from lack of sun. Piper wondered how it was that no one had claimed the throne from this weak-looking creature. In her days, she had met – and sometimes bedded – monarchs far more vigorous.

She cleared her throat. "King Willburn? There is something you need to say to me."

The creature in the throne moved ever so slowly, as if trying to hide the movement even from himself. "Where are you going, Road's Beloved?"

Piper shrugged. "I go where my feet carry me. They seem about to carry me somewhere useful to you."

"Come closer and let me look at you."

Piper obeyed. A gnarled old finger reached for her arm, and she permitted it. He traced a past journey that she remembered well, a stretch of road that wound around a cliffside slippery with ocean spray. Her footing on that road had been uncertain, and it had carried her into a cave empty only at low tide. There, an ancient merman had whispered secrets in her ear, gifts for a long-lost daughter born to a vivacious ship's captain whose home lay hundreds of miles away along the coast. As a dry fingernail scraped her flesh, Piper recalled watching lightning scratch the surface of the sky as the ocean waves eddied around her ankles. She'd walked half in a dream for days, wrestling with new images of what the sun did during the night and what became of bodies once they drifted to the ocean floor and where the largest pearls in the ocean lay and what guarded them.

"You have been on many journeys in your time," the King said in a reedy voice.

"I think of it as one very long journey."

"I recognize some of your marks. A road far, far south of Sharksbay." He touched her other arm. "A path that seems to lead up to heaven itself."

Piper stepped back, shaken for the first time in a while. "How would you know such things?"

"I've made a study of what it is to be a Road's Beloved. Cut the skin off more than a few. Stretched and dried it, bound it in books. It gave me time to identify the roads they'd walked and learn their stories, to understand what gave Worldsbridge its name." The childish singsong of his voice horrified Piper absolutely.

"The Road would never stand for–"

"The Road is no kind master. You must know at least that, girl."

"The Road has granted me strong magic."

King Willburn laughed, his mirth pulling his lips away from long, strong white teeth. "If I wished to flay you as well, you could not stop me."

Piper marked exits – the way she'd come, of course, and a window that might open to the other side of the palace. "You have a message?"

"Oh yes, I do. It's for the Road itself."

"For the Road?" Piper echoed. She hated herself for having been carefree just moments before. She had entered the city so casually, made love to the guard so arrogantly, walked into the palace like a person sure to survive.

"It's unseemly to behave as if you haven't heard me when you have."

"I can't give a message to the Road. There's no one to talk to, nowhere to go."

"You poor darling. Covered with maps, a living embodiment of the Road's whim, and you haven't figured out that the Road is something – someone – real. Someone you can touch and talk to. Someone who can make mistakes and perhaps be killed. Someone who supposedly loves you. Someone who can lie."

The King's lips writhed like worms as he spoke, seeming to twist around themselves. Piper tore her gaze away. The sight of them felt too vulgar, too intimate. She glanced around the room, noted that the windows were perfectly aligned with the cardinal directions. The sun was setting in the west, its orange-red light making the flesh of the man in the throne appear fevered.

She cleared her throat, straightened her body. "What is

your message for the Road?" She would figure out how to deliver a message to the Road itself once she got away from this mad king and shook the dust of this place off her feet.

His fingers dipped into his robes and emerged with a long, thin tube. "It's just some questions I've been wondering about. I ask the Road: Do you care at all for those you mark *Beloved*? How do we know?" He lifted the tube to his lips and exhaled sharply.

Piper didn't move in time to avoid the dart. It bit her throat sharper than a horsefly. An ominous, cool stillness chased the pain and began to spread into her lungs.

The King laughed dryly. "I ask you, *Beloved One*, what drives you to the next step, the next Road? Do you tire? Do you ever wish to stop?"

She struggled to catch her breath, but felt oddly compelled to answer him. "There is a restlessness–"

"And the Road makes wonderful use of that, no? I wonder what it would take to make the Road come for you? What would have to happen to you? How much would you have to hurt?"

Piper tried to whirl toward the west-facing window opposite the King, but her feet tripped each other and she fell to the floor instead. Two more darts struck her, one in the ankle and one in the upper arm. She feared the numbness that rippled from their points of contact. "Stop. Please."

"Perhaps I'll simply keep you here. If you never take another step on the Road planned for you, what does it matter?"

Another voice, both familiar and strange, sounded from the grand doors to the throne room. "Enough."

Piper squinted toward the source of the voice. She saw two bodies, superimposed on each other. She knew one rather well – the lush and powerful form of the city guard Etta. The other was tall as a late evening shadow, skin sun-baked, carrying the scents of spices of distant marketplaces and the wet, fertile earth from the thickest jungle and much more besides. Piper shook her head, trying to clear it of whatever the King had used to drug her.

"It's you, isn't it? You do care about this one?" The King's voice contained a whine.

The two forms split apart. One – Etta – ran to Piper and caught her in powerful arms. Piper felt fingers stroking back hair that had somehow become sweat-soaked, then plucking out the needles in her throat, arm and ankle.

The other stepped toward the King. "You thought to gain my attention through betrayal."

"You came to me once," the King said. "I remember the night it happened." He slammed a fist against the arm of his throne.

"You were very special to me then," the figure said. "I gave you much more than most."

"No one could be satisfied with your gifts," spat the King.

"The way of the Road has little to do with satisfaction."

Piper accepted Etta's help struggling to her feet. Etta's warm breath touched her ear. "Maybe you don't know as much as you thought, eh?" Despite the chastisement, the voice was gentle and full of humor.

"I was an ass," Piper murmured. "I'm very glad to see you."

"Look at this," Etta whispered, turning over her wrist. At the spot where the veins approached the surface most closely was a thick black X, and tendrils of Road curled away from it toward the red-brown expanses of the rest of her body.

Piper touched the center of the X, a thought tugging at her mind.

"Are you satisfied with me now?" the King asked, spreading his arms grandly. His voice gained strength and echoed, commanding the attention of all in the room. The blankets fell away from his hands and forearms as he moved, and Piper saw that highways and byways etched his skin, a map so thick with Roads past and present that it put even hers to shame. "I am my own man."

"I gave you pathways almost infinite in their variety..." the tall stranger said.

"And I have chosen not to walk them. I came to Worldsbridge, the place where all roads meet, and I sat at this crossroads and have not moved since. They extended the palace to shelter me because I am their King."

"Crossroads..." Piper murmured. She traced the X on Etta's arm. The sun slipped further, and the red-orange light began to fade to purple. The tall stranger grew brighter in the shadows. Piper, staring at his back, felt suddenly as if she knew him, recognized the compulsion that sometimes came over her to rush after a person in a crowd and tug at his shoulder. The impulse was nearly always wrong, but it spoke to the power of a familiar gesture in a foreign place, the trick of the light that made a stranger seem to be a friend. Quickly and softly in Etta's ear, Piper whispered, "I think this is a place of power. What did you see when you went outside the city?"

"I'd not gone three steps beyond the walls before that stranger came to me. He said it was not yet time for me to walk away from you, and I already knew that. It made sense when he took my hand and we followed you."

"The Road is not made for sitting still," the stranger said, his voice angry as thunder.

"You said that to me the night you came," the King said. He dropped his well-traveled arms back to his lap and became small again. "It was raining that night and I'd sought shelter under a tree. You goaded me into racing you through the mud."

"It was a lesson and a warning. Stillness has ever been your enemy, Will. Remember how the rain lost its chill when we ran and found the joy in it?"

"I twisted my ankle in the mud."

"Did I not soothe it?"

"You never let me rest."

"Rest comes in fits and starts along a journey, and if you feel you've had enough of it, more likely, you've had too much."

"Your way is cruel, and I am tired," screamed the King. Despite his ancient appearance, he moved his arms like a small child having a tantrum.

The stranger shook his head. He turned to Piper and Etta. His eyes glinted like the lights of a city glimpsed on the farthest horizon. "Come closer, my beloved."

Etta helped Piper approach him. Piper stared into the strange and familiar face. She recognized the hills and valleys of it. "It's true," she said. "You are the Road. You are someone."

"It may be better to say I am some*thing*, but it is true that you can touch and speak to me."

He pulled them to his side. Piper's heart soared in his presence. King Willburn was not wrong, for the Road was cruel. Many times in her travels, she had feared for her life. Many times, she had walked through bleeding calluses and broken hopes. However, the Road was never without a horizon, never without the dream of what might wait around the next corner. Adventure, tragedy, friend or foe – the Road ever promised change, and for as long as Piper could remember, she had wanted that.

The Road reached out to Etta with his left hand and to Piper with his right. They all faced King Willburn. "You come to me also," said the Road. "You are still my beloved, Will."

The King's knees, ankles and hips cracked audibly as he rose. Blankets fell away like glaciers begrudgingly shifting off the land. The King was taller than he seemed, younger than he'd first appeared. "I hate you," he said, but stepped forward.

"You have asked many questions," said the Road. "Now I ask all of you: What becomes of a man who refuses to travel the Road laid out before him?"

"Nothing," said Piper, understanding something of the King and his palace and the city around it.

"Death," said King Willburn, refusing to make eye contact with any of them.

"Everything changes," Etta said. "The world goes on, and whoever does not walk is left behind."

The Road lifted Etta's arm as if she were the victor of a race. "Yes, my darling. I am so glad Piper found you for us. That is exactly right." He released Piper and Etta and reached for King Willburn. The King twisted, parts of his body moving away from the stranger's hands and parts yearning toward them. Ultimately, he did not seem able to resist, and the stranger pulled the King into an embrace, traced marks so thick they wound around his ears and under his hair.

"You've been foolish, Will. You can't dry the skin of a Road's Beloved and think you've made a map. My beloved carry maps on living flesh because my flesh is living, and the Road is living. It breathes and changes with each new day, just as your toe became crooked as you walked and you grew a beard and shaved it off again. You've cursed yourself, do you see?"

"My maps are wrong now."

"All of them. You've twisted them. And it will be a long time walking before they start to become true again."

"No!" King Willburn cried, wrenching himself away. "No! I am *tired*. You can't make me." He stumbled to the edges of the room, half-hid himself behind a suit of armor, fumbled as if to take its weapon.

"What say you?" the Road asked Etta. "Can I make him walk?"

"No," she replied. "But it will not go well for him if he does not make himself."

"And why is that?"

Etta glanced at Piper, almost as if looking for permission. Piper met her gaze, but understood that this moment was for Etta. The markings of the Road had appeared on Etta for a reason, and they had taken their own shape. Piper's path had crossed Etta's for a purpose, but Etta now possessed a map of her own.

Etta stepped toward the throne. King Willburn howled and rushed at her, but Etta was a city guard. Her foot shot out nimbly and sent him sprawling face-first. She lifted him by the scruff of his neck like a mother lioness lifting a cub. There was no mistaking the fear on his face as she studied him.

"What are you going to do to me?" King Willburn asked, and Piper noticed the submission in his tone, as if he already knew something that she was still only beginning to realize.

The throne room was all shadow now, the sun having ended its day's work and disappeared into the secrets of the night. At first, it seemed the only light was from the Road, an odd glint here and there from his eyes or his teeth. Soon, Piper realized that something else was glowing – the X on Etta's wrist, and every scrap of Road that flowed from it.

"I am the Queen of this Crossroads now, the Queen of Worldsbridge," Etta said, "by the power of the Road that has led me to this place. It is not for me to do anything to you – it is for you to choose. A crossroads is a place of choices, and you have always known this. It is understandable to sit for a day and a night, to ponder. But we all know that if you sit still at a crossroads long enough, devils come to tempt you. And any choice unmade too long has a way of making itself." She set King Willburn down and tore the shirt from him, revealing more unwalked and outdated roads.

"The choices?"

"We have just laid them out, and you have always known them."

"Nothing, death or walking into the dark."

"Yes, and King Willburn – you understand by now, I hope, that *nothing* is the most terrible choice of all."

Piper thought perhaps she recognized the mountain range that moved up and down his throat when he swallowed. The Road reached out a hand and touched the side of the King's face. "Will, if you are truly so tired, there can be honor in death."

"No!" He shook himself away, pressed himself back from all of them. "You are a liar. You say you love and you don't. You said you would see me again and you never came back."

"I am here now, am I not? Simply because it isn't the way you imagined–"

"No! Don't speak to me and don't touch me." He turned

to Etta and spat, "I hope that throne swallows you as it did me. You say you give me a choice, but truly, you have left me none. Walking into the terror of the darkness. It's what the Road always planned for me."

Piper felt moved in a way she had not expected, despite the continuing sting from where he had struck her with darts. "Willburn. We could walk together for a time if you wish."

"You think you're better than me, but just wait. Spend three more lonely seasons along the seaside. Or walk with none to speak to but the eagles. See what happens to you then. See if later you understand the urge to just sit down for a time." He tore open the west window and plunged out of it as if going to chase the sun.

They all stared after him. "He is not well," the Road said.

"There's nothing you can do for him?" Piper asked. "Aren't you some sort of god?"

The tall stranger's lips turned with a bitter laugh. "You mortals always misunderstand where the powers of gods begin and end. You are the one thing we can't control." As he said it, he faded, and Piper knew that she would continue to glimpse him for the rest of her life, just as she always had – though there was no telling if they would ever meet or speak in such a way again.

Piper wondered if the long walk ahead would heal Willburn – sometimes, a long walk had healed her. Long walks, however, had also given her heartbreak and scars – and, if she looked into uncomfortable corners of herself, a belief that nothing and no one truly mattered, a willingness to use people.

Etta had taken her new place on the throne. Piper

approached and went to one knee. “Queen. Etta. I will remember your name and much more.”

Etta’s hand darted out to brush Piper’s shoulder, her fingers no longer shy. “What was it you said when you arrived? The ruler of this place has a message for you?”

Piper blushed. She felt as if she’d been years younger then, though she’d entered the city only a short time before. “I did say a thing like that.”

“Perhaps you were mistaken about which ruler had the message. I think it is I, not Willburn. And I think the message is for you to carry in your heart and keep for yourself.”

Piper nodded and then kept her head bowed, humbled. “I am ready to hear it.”

“A Road is not a simple line. It may be true that it never crosses itself or doubles back, but this does not mean that one who walks it will never return to the same place. One who believes such a thing has forgotten the nature of circles – and the nature of Roads, and the nature of people.”

“When did you learn these things? When did you know you would be Queen?”

“I think you chose me and then the Road chose me because I understand something about learning as I go.” Etta stood up from the throne and reached for Piper’s arm. “This throne won’t swallow me if I stand up from it from time to time. If I’m reading what’s written on my skin correctly, my way involves learning the paths that lead to and from this place.”

She was so lovely and powerful, and also regal. Piper stepped closer until they brushed against each other and saw that she could still make Etta blush.

Willburn had asked: *Does the Road care at all for those who have been marked Beloved? How do we know?* Piper held the answer now in her heart, and it comforted her. *Because we may not be given the gift of rest, but we never run out of Road, so we are never abandoned. More Road means more chances.* She laced her fingers with Etta's and stepped forward toward the next.

AUTHOR'S NOTE

I've been thinking about the Road's Beloved for about 20 years, but I could never decide how to execute the story. Did the story exist in an entirely different world? Was this urban fantasy? Is there one Road's Beloved or are there many?

Finally, I just wanted to tell the story. When I started to write about Piper, I realized I'd found my way to a rich vein and that it can't and shouldn't be limited. As further stories revealed, the Road's Beloved concept works best when I say *yes* to every question. Where can a Road's Beloved be? *Anywhere there is a road.* What is a road? *A road can take many forms.*

As of this writing, I already know that Piper's journeys aren't limited to Worldsbridge. She'll make her way into many places and times, some of which cross into the history of our timeline. I quickly realized that a woman with so many roads to travel is going to go wherever she wants.

In giving myself permission to write this way, I'm indebted to Michael Moorcock's concept of the Eternal

Champion. I remember the wonder I felt when I realized the true breadth of what the Eternal Champion meant to Moorcock, and I feel the same type of wonder when I think or write about the Road's Beloved now.

Thank you for reading this first story about Piper and the Road's Beloved – it won't be the last. I hope you'll continue to travel beside me.

- Erica Anoe, January 2022

ACKNOWLEDGMENTS

First and foremost, thank you for reading.

Thank you to Elizabeth, for many things – reading the first draft, loving the story, making a beautiful cover and being so interested in Piper.

Thank you to Lonely Robot Press for creating a beautiful edition of this story.

Thank you to Dean Wesley Smith for reminding me to have fun with my writing and for the amazing book *Writing Into the Dark*. Piper emerged immediately the moment I let go and went along for the ride with the creative voice.

Thank you to Paul for being patient with the time I spend telling Piper's stories and for listening to me reading random snippets out loud.

Thank you to the Road. While I can't formally claim to be a Road's Beloved, I always felt like the Road kinda liked me.

ABOUT THE AUTHOR

Erica Anoe is a hapa haole writer who is interested in exploring characters and places that exist on the borderlands. Born in Kailua, Hawai'i, she currently lives on the mainland and works in cybersecurity.

ALSO BY ERICA ANOE

Coming Soon

Hawaiian Football Blues: A Road's Beloved Short Story

Piper's next adventure is an urban fantasy story set in the seedy underbelly of 1970s Hawaii. Visit Lonely Robot Press for more information.

Historical Fiction:

Trapped in the Hold of the SS Madras: A Kingdom of Hawai'i Short Story

"We were not sick with smallpox, but we knew we would be soon if we couldn't get out of this hold."

April 1883. The SS Madras arrives at the port of Honolulu with hundreds of workers for the rice paddies of Waikiki – but it also carries smallpox. Historical fiction set in the waters of the Kingdom of Hawai'i, "Trapped in the Hold of the SS Madras" tells the story of a steamer mired in uncertainty, a kingdom determined to avoid another plague, and passengers desperate to disembark before they contract a deadly disease.

Includes a historical note by the author with information about the case heard by the Supreme Court of the Kingdom of Hawai'i that inspired this story.

www.ingramcontent.com/pod-product-compliance
Lightning Source LLC
La Vergne TN
LVHW020537160826
845677LV00015B/4119

* 9 7 9 8 4 2 0 9 8 7 9 1 9 *